PARSONS GREEN NURSERY CL
AUGUST '98

MY BEST FRIEND

Pat Hutchins

MY BEST FRIEND

RED FOX

A Red Fox Book

Published by Random House Children's Books
20 Vauxhall Bridge Road, London SW1V 2SA

A division of Random House UK Ltd
London Melbourne Sydney Auckland
Johannesburg and agencies throughout the world

Copyright © 1993 Pat Hutchins

3 5 7 9 10 8 6 4

First published in the USA 1993 by Greenwillow Books
First published in Great Britain 1993 by Julia MacRae

Red Fox edition 1995

Printed in China

RANDOM HOUSE UK Limited Reg. No. 954009

ISBN 0 09 928191 0

FOR

HARRY

POLLY

BEVERLEY

JULIE

JANIS

DAVID

EILEEN

SUE

HELEN

KAREN

CAROL

JUDITH

JENNY

ELLEN

ANDREW

AND ESPECIALLY

CLARA JANE OF LUMB BANK

My best friend is coming
to stay the night.
I'm glad she's my best friend.

My best friend knows how to run faster

and climb higher

and jump further than anyone.

I'm glad she's my best friend.

My best friend can eat spaghetti with a fork and doesn't drop any on the table.

My best friend knows how to paint good pictures and doesn't get fingermarks on the paper.

My best friend knows
how to untie her shoelaces

and how to do up the buttons on her pyjamas.

My best friend knows how to read.

I'm glad she's my best friend.

My best friend thinks
there's a monster in the room.

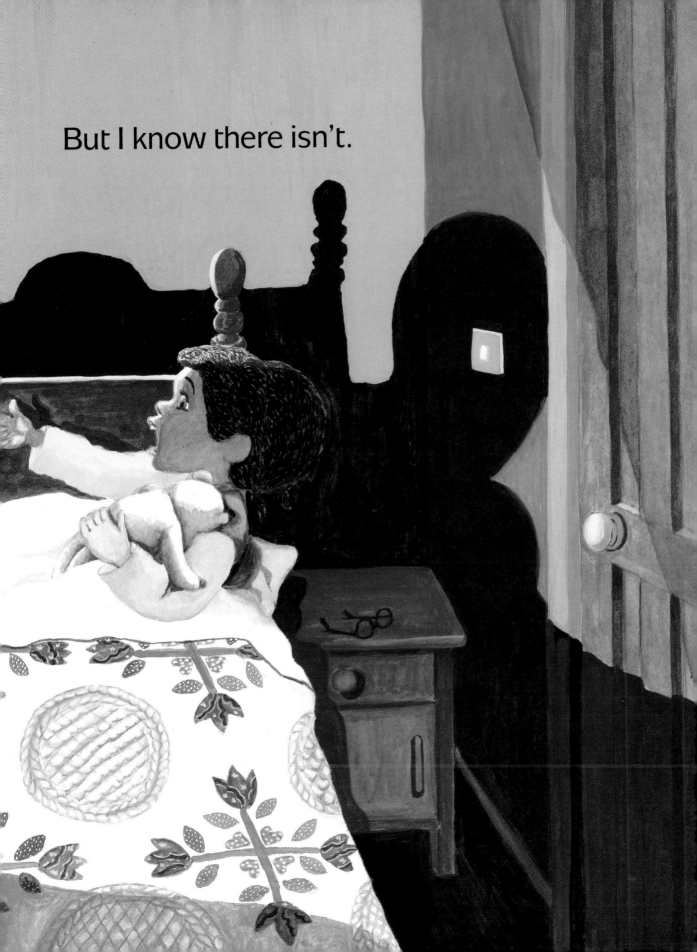

I know it's only the wind blowing the curtains.

And I know if I close the window,
the curtains won't blow.

"I'm glad you're my best friend,"
said my best friend.

Since the publication of *Rosie's Walk* in 1968, reviewers on both sides of the Atlantic have been loud in their praise of Pat Hutchins's work. Among her popular picture books are *Tidy Titch; What Game Shall We Play?; Where's the Baby?*; *The Doorbell Rang* ; and *The Wind Blew* (winner of the 1974 Kate Greenaway Medal). For older readers she has written several novels, including *The House That Sailed Away, The Curse of the Egyptian Mummy,* and *Rats!* Pat Hutchins, her husband, Laurence, and their sons, Morgan and Sam, live in London.